Miss Daisy

Fred Grace

Published by:

Technicraft/MusicExplorers

York, PA

USA

i

Storyline

This "long" short story or Novelette (13,100 words) is about an attractive middle-aged woman living in a mid-western state who had fallen in love in her youth but lost her one and only love. She had become despondent and had given up all hope of finding what she once had. As she wonders about town the town's people refer to her as "Miss Daisy." A hardened newspaper reporter from New York happened to be dispatched to her small town to cover a story about a young upstart politician. While there, this younger reporter encounters the woman and her unhappiness. Through his persistent efforts, she regains happiness and love. The events related to his helping her changes him significantly. He develops a new sense of compassion and understanding that was foreign to his earlier nature. Miss Daisy is forever grateful to the reporter for restoring her happiness.

Dedication

This book is dedicated to my immediate family:

My beautiful wife Elaine,
Our beautiful children, their spouses, and our grandchildren:
Jennifer Grace Wildasin, Aaron and Nicole Wildasin,
Laureen Grace Sahoo, Purush and Joshua Sahoo,
Gregory, Sharon, Brian and Jordan Grace,
Stephen and Lisa Goodling,
Craig and Daniel Goodling and Roxie Gratton.

Copyright © 2017 by Fred Grace

ISBN-13: 978-0-9975513-1-0
ISBN-10: 0997551313

Visit: www.musicexplorers.com

Chapter 1. The Matches

"Fault," cried the line judge as Lenard's serve struck wide of the sideline. He knew that he had a chance to win this match if his next serve could be swift and placed within play. The match had been grueling and fiercely fought as the two traded serves followed by seemingly endless volleys.

Lenard's best serve was cross-court and to the sideline. The ball seemed to jump as it struck so as to make return of his serve very difficult. That was his strong point and if he were to win this match he likely would have to rely on one of his best serves ever. The two had traded sets with Lenard winning the first set, his opponent winning the second set and now they were tied at six games each in the third set.

Fred Grace

Lenard's mind began to drift. He was thinking about two days earlier when he had faced his opponent David in the district mixed doubles championship match. He and his partner Susan took on David and Lillian. While they represented Springdale High, David and Lillian were from Maytown High, a school in a small neighboring town within this mid-western State.

Lenard, a senior, and Susan, a junior, were expected to win this battle, but Lenard had difficulty focusing on the game. He and Susan had won the first set 6-3 but now were falling behind in the second set 3-5.

Lenard did not recall seeing Lillian in any previous matches with Maytown. He knew David as a tennis player well. They had been each other's nemesis over the past several years. But he was sure he had not seen Lillian before, and could not keep his eyes off of her. In the midst of the ongoing second set, Lenard began to realize that his unforced errors had something to do with this beautiful, athletic young woman on the opposite side of the court.

Lillian was about five foot three and her body was a mixture of athleticism and femininity. She was neat and trim and a very attractive young woman. She moved smoothly back and forth across the court, was agile, and had quick responses. She was youthful and full of life. She definitely was an outstanding young woman and beautiful as well.

Lenard knew he was being distracted by Lillian and attempted to guard against it to little avail. David and Lillian came back winning the next two sets 6-4 and 6-4. Maytown in the persons of Lillian and David won the district mixed doubles championship.

After the match, Lenard gathered up his gear and proceeded across the street from the tennis court for some refreshments. To his delight he came across Lillian sitting by herself outside and having a soda at a table in front of the drug store. "Hello Lillian," he said as he introduced himself as Lennard Trussel a bit awkwardly as if she really didn't know who he was. This was the first time that they had spoken to each other. She responded with "Hello Lenard." "Congratulations on your well-deserved victory," he offered. Lillian smiled and responded "Thank you. You know that you and Susan made the match very competitive. You are both very good players. I am surprised that we won."

By then, Lillian seemed to be getting somewhat anxious about them being alone together, which was not understood by Lenard until he saw David approaching. He had noticed David's overprotection during set breaks and surmised that David had more than just a friendly interest in her. But he wasn't sure of her interest in David. It seemed as if she was somewhat standoffish toward David at times. But yet she seemed comforted to have him nearby as well.

Perhaps that's the way things were in a small town back then with so few people that the dating game had little options. As Lenard left the two, he couldn't help thinking of how exciting it had been to interact with Lillian but also with such few words spoken he could not read any response from her except cordiality. Lenard would have to wait until the Award Ceremonies and the Dance that followed to get a better idea of what his chances with Lillian might be.

Fred Grace

Lenard met Susan at the car in the parking lot. "I'm sorry Susan. I think I let you down in the match." "Well Lenard, we all have good days and not so good days." "I guess you are right," he responded, "Let's go home, relax for a while, and then have some light practice to get you ready for tomorrow." Susan agreed.

The woman's singles championship match was being held that next morning. Susan was the top seed in the district and was at the top of her game. She was athletic and powerful, had great moves, and was good on her feet. She had practiced against Lenard regularly and was used to powerful play.

Susan's opponent was a fierce competitor named Ruby, a redhead, and a senior from Stockbury High, who had a most powerful serve and essentially got to the district championship game relying on that asset. She had narrowly defeated Lillian by scores of 6-4, 4-6, and 6-4. But the win earned her the spot in the championship match.

Susan and Ruby took the court. Susan had been used to swift serves and was able to return these with relatively little trouble. She also was able to place the ball on the court from side to side in such a manner to move her opponent back and forth until she could no longer reach the volleys. In two straight sets, Susan won the woman's district championship, 6-4 and 6-3.

After the match, Susan returned from the locker room to meet Lenard who was waiting near the court exit to the parking lot. "Congratulations Susan, Wow, what a match!" he exclaimed. Susan responded "Well, I couldn't have won without your help. Thank you Lenard, I will always be grateful to you." And with that she gave Lenard a long hug. As they stood together, Susan reveled in the accolades that were offered by spectators that were leaving the court area.

Seemingly out of nowhere Ruby appeared on the scene. She had deliberately wandered over to where they were standing. "Congratulation on coaching Susan so well," she stated, as if Susan wasn't there at all. Ruby was an attractive girl with flashy blue-green eyes, light skin, and divine body shape. And Lenard seemed to be relishing in her attention. "Could we stop by the drug store for a soda?" she asked.

But Susan read her interest in Lenard as an intrusion. Before he could provide an answer, Susan urged "Lenard, I think we should be going on our way. You need to be relaxing before the men's singles match tomorrow." "Yes," agreed Lenard. Then with a certain smile that said perhaps we will meet again soon, Lenard bade farewell to Ruby and headed to the car.

Until yesterday, he had a genuine interest in Ruby and had looked forward to her appearance at the tournament. But, Lillian had captured his attention far more than anyone else before, and his newly found interest had pushed Ruby nearly totally out of his thoughts.

As he walked along with Susan, he mused to himself that Susan's fear was unfounded since he only had a casual interest in Ruby at this moment. He did not feel obligated to tell Susan about his newly found interest in Lillian.

That was then. Right now, Lenard was in the battle of his tennis life against David, who was not without his own prowess. He had beaten Lenard on several occasions and truly had a wicked serve. But by this match, Lenard had figured him out and was ready.

The match was being fiercely fought and with a little luck either man could win. David was about five foot ten, had smooth moves, and could scamper from one side of the court to the other as quickly as a cat. Lenard was an inch taller and not quite so agile but had a powerful upper body. Both were handsome in their own respects. David was talkative and outgoing while Lenard was reserved, confident, but not so talkative.

As the match wore on, it became increasingly clear that someone would have to blow their chances and lose or have some extremely good luck to win the match. Each had ample opportunities to win the match outright, but also were able to keep each other off guard just enough to keep the match going.

Over two hours had gone by and both men were exhausted. The match was in a tiebreaker. But during the course of the last two sets, Lenard noticed that his opponent was returning his best serve more than expected. Not only that, he was placing the ball down the sideline and deep toward the baseline where Lenard was unable to get to it. Several times he attempted to let up on that serve but still the ball was being returned. The tiebreaker went back and forth from duce to advantage with both taking the lead and both falling behind.

MISS DAISY

In his aggressive attempt to win and end the game, Lenard's opponent double faulted during his service. Advantage Lenard. Now was Lenard's chance to win the match and end play. He decided to place his serve along the opposite side this time even though it was by no means his best serve nor had it been that effective today.

As he tossed the ball in the air, he brought his racket down swiftly and almost with reckless abandon. The ball rocketed off the sweet spot and caught his opponent leaning the wrong way as it hit just inside the centerline. It was an Ace! "Game, Set and Match" declared the umpire. Lenard had won the district conference singles tennis crown and was the champion! He consoled his opponent David and placed his arm around him as they headed for the locker room.

Chapter 2. Why Maytown?

"Where is J. P.?" Watson shouted. "In his office" was the reply. "I want him in here immediately!" I rounded the corner and proceeded into Watson's office. "J. P., I want you to cover a story in Maytown." "What about the senator scandal in Albany?" I stated. "Forget that, we are behind on that story anyhow."

"Where in the heck is Maytown?" I inquired. "In the mid-western part of the country," was the answer. "Why?" I asked. "There is a young man there who is an upstart politician and I want to beat everybody to the punch. He may be President of the country someday, and I want to be in on it before the very start. And I need to put my best man on this case." "Good Lord," I thought to myself, "Why do I need to be his best man at this very moment."

That was Watson's way. It seemed he'd get these wild goose ride ideas and send me on wild goose chases after them. My thoughts went back to the time he sent me to Chantly in the Deep South. I spent an eternity there in just a few days.

"But I have tickets to the Yankees and Tigers games for the coming weekend," I protested. "Thank you, my boy," was Watson's response. "I've been wanting to take my wife to the ball park for some time." With that, I knew I couldn't win.

Watson was a short overweight man with burly thick eyebrows and thinning disheveled hair. One might take him for an ogre until you got to know him. He was full of life and generous to his employees but also liked to see them squirm as he dished out assignments. But he knew how to let up when the situation demanded it.

He knew the newspaper business and had been around the block many times. He exercised good judgement and assigned duties based on his insight regarding capabilities of the individual. He seemed to relish making assignments that would not be of liking but he would fully support the effort as needed. He knew that I did not want any part of this aggravating duty.

After our discussion, I went home and prepared for the trip. Reluctantly, I packed my bags and took a taxi to the train station. There I bought a ticket to Bennington which was the largest city in the Midwest area, aside from Chicago. It would be about a three-hour drive from there to Maytown.

After entering the train, I took a seat on the north side so the sun would not be shinning in my eyes as I gazed out the window. As if that really mattered because I wasn't interested in the lay of the land or scenery anyhow. As the train passed along and into the countryside, it seemed as if we were disappearing into an abyss and far from civilization. This kind of excursion from my usual comfortable existence was exactly why I did not like these kinds of assignments.

After arriving at Bennington, I rented a car and drove to Maytown. When I had asked directions to the Maytown Hotel, they said that once I got to town, I couldn't miss it. How right they were! In such small town it seemed that about the only pretense of existence was indeed the Hotel itself.

I proceeded to the front desk to get a room. In the lobby sat an older man reading a newspaper and as I stood there waiting for the hotel clerk to check me in, the old man peered over the top and was sizing me up. Obviously, I was a stranger to this town, the likes of which seldom seen.

A middle-aged lady was waiting in the lobby sitting by her suitcase and ready to be picked up by taxi, I presumed. Several people walked past me through the lobby on their way to the cafe. As they passed by they smiled and nodded as if to say good-day and then continued on their way. I observed others passing by but had little idea of what they were up to or where they were going.

After some time, he asked "A room for one or two?" "One," I replied. "For how many nights?" "Three, maybe four," I stated. "Alright, here is the key – Room 206. Will that be ok?" "Yes," I replied. "If you have a need for anything, just let us know – dial zero to get the front desk." "Thanks," I responded, "I believe everything should be ok." "Would you like your bags delivered to your room, Sir?" "No thanks. I'll take them myself."

After entering the room, I noticed that the Hotel was old but accommodating, much like a lot of old Hotels I had frequented in the city. But here everything was laid out almost perfectly, even if it really didn't have to be. As I was taking in the surroundings, a knock came on the door. A maid announced that she had new linen and fresh towels. I left her in and she diligently went about placing everything in order, didn't say anything, and then left.

I remember seeing old movies where such service was the case in cites large or small. That was no longer the custom elsewhere. I thought this place has a certain bit of charm left over from the old days, but beyond that I knew I was going to be terribly bored until I got back home.

In many respects this town seemed far too quaint, and although accommodating, seemed to be left in the last century. And the people seemed a bit strange to me as if somehow they were wound up, let go, and mechanically went about their business. They were not shouting, yelling, pushing, or in each other's face. There were no car pile ups in the streets with honking horns and unruly drivers. It was as if they simply lacked emotion, passion, heart and soul, and went about as robots.

I had similar experiences in other places like Chantly that I had visited. But I was not interested in charm, I was living at a fast pace and didn't have time or patience for all of that. My inclination was to get my story covered and get out of here as soon as possible.

After freshening up, I proceeded down to the lounge, which appeared to be one, albeit small, of the social centers of town. An older couple was having drinks and there was a young couple sitting quietly, smiling at each other, and hardly talking. I supposed that was the way it is in these parts when couples enjoy each other's company.

Some local guys of about my age were having their own fun over toward the corner, smoking cigars, drinking beer, and laughing it up. I thought to myself that at least somebody here was actively pursuing life.

I could overhear their talk but couldn't make any sense of their local stories or jokes. It seemed as if they were stuck in this town and had never even traveled to the next county. Certainly, we had something in common since I felt stuck here as well, if only for a few days. I sat there having a drink as I contemplated tomorrow's activity, my plan for covering the story and connecting with the young politician.

As the afternoon wore down, I found myself alone. My thoughts bounced around to wondering what kind of backwoodsman would be running for political office, the ensuing interview with him, and the town itself. Sarcastically, I doubted if he were to be anything but a woefully far cry from another Abraham Lincoln. Also, I wondered how I was supposed to write a story having real interest to people who inhabited the civilized parts of the country.

Beyond that, I thought about where and when I'd have dinner. The smell emanating from the hotel dining room was reasonably inviting so I decided to try it but since it was too early to eat, I had another drink.

Then, unexpectedly, an extremely attractive woman of about my age came in. It appeared to me that she had been on a trip and was wanting to unwind before going home. I took notice that she had no ring on her finger, so I felt free to approach her, as if that ever mattered to me before.

Back in the city, I never dated much, for mostly I traveled a lot and just didn't have time to establish any long term relationships. Even then, my callous nature had often ended any possibilities. And I didn't really understand women, nor did I care to try. But when traveling, I met quite a few women and had learned how to make an impression, have a few intimate moments, and end it there when I left.

She sat a few stools away and ordered a drink. I turned toward her and said "Looks like you've had a rough day." She explained that she just got back from a trip, was exhausted, and apologized for her looks. I took her apology as a sign of insecurity because although she appeared tired, she literally looked like a fashion plate.

I continued chatting with her, figuring that I might be able use her to find out more about the town as a backdrop for my story. Perhaps she knew something about the young politician. She offered her name as Vivian. Although she was well groomed and polished, she certainly was not nearly as sophisticated as women in New York City.

Vivian agreed to dinner and we talked about Maytown and her career as a traveling sales agent for a small fashion company near Chicago. Her ambition was to make it as an aspiring woman in the fashion world in the big city. I thought "good luck lady. The sharks at that level will eat you alive."

She was impressed that I was there covering a story about the upstart politician but really didn't know him since she had moved there only recently from another small town in the state. As we left the hotel restaurant she handed me a slip that contained her name, address, and telephone number and asked me to keep in touch. When I got to my room, I crinkled up the paper and callously discarded it. The last thing I needed was a long-distance relationship with a woman living in the wilderness.

Chapter 3. The Dance

Lenard picked Susan up at her home on the way to the award ceremonies and the dance that would follow. "Glad to see you are ready, my dear," Lenard stated. "You look gorgeous this evening, Susan." Susan lit up with delight. "Oh Lenard, you are such a good talker and very handsome man," she responded. "Are you ready to receive your trophy," Lenard kidded. "Oh yes, and I can't wait to see you get yours too. This is a great night for Springdale," she added.

As Lenard and Susan entered the building, Susan left to visit the powder room. Just then Ruby appeared on her way to the main room where the ceremonies were being held. She was dressed in a long rather tight red gown that was very revealing. "Hi Lenard," she stated as she came to Lenard and stood very close to him.

Lenard was well aware that this beauty was very interested in him. And she was very attractive. Her perfume and closeness told him she was indeed a fine woman. But Lenard had his own thoughts. They were focused on Lillian. He could think of no one else.

Lenard responded with "Hello Ruby, you look great tonight." "Thank you Lenard, I was hoping you would like my gown. You may ask me for a dance later on this evening." "Yes, I just might do that," he responded, "after the ceremonies." It was his way of saying "perhaps" without saying "no." He watched Ruby as she walked away exaggerating her every move. He was unaware that Lillian had been watching this encounter.

When Susan returned, they entered the main room to appear at the formalities before the dance. He was dressed in a grey sport coat, black slacks, and a white turtle neck sweater, and she wore a bright green gown. Susan being a beauty and Lenard being handsome made for a very attractive couple. They were seated at a table just in front of the main table of dignitaries.

After some time Lenard's eyes moved quickly across the room and found Lillian. His mind was focused on Lillian and knew that he would be totally engrossed in thoughts about her during the remainder of the evening. As he watched her, he saw her for the first time in something other than tennis attire or casual clothes. He was truly impressed by her beauty and grace.

These district award ceremonies were huge in this part of the state. They established bragging rights for the townspeople, where not much else took place during the year to cheer about.

As David and Lillian took the stage for their award, Lenard could not help thinking that he would gladly give up his award if Lillian had been his doubles partner and they would have won the doubles championship trophy together. He envied David at this moment.

The next award was presented to Susan for being the ladies' singles champion. Subsequently, Lenard accepted his trophy thanked his supporters and the commission that had held the matches.

The ceremony seemed to go on endlessly, with various speakers from the commission, Maytown, Springdale, and Stockbury covering past historical events related to the tennis greats of yore, delving into historical foundations of their respective towns, and covering every aspect of the lives of the competitors. The town officials were went on and on glorying in victory.

Lenard, being a man of lesser words, was totally bored with all of that, although he enjoyed recognition for his accomplishment. His defeat of David had now taken on new meaning. Not only was he the best male tennis player in the district but also he was hoping that his triumph over David would have a positive effect on Lillian. Aside from that he just wanted the ceremony to end.

After the long dragged-out affair, the dance began. It was traditional that with the first dance, the mixed doubles participants would dance with their double's partner. Lenard slid gracefully across the floor with Susan in his arms. Her stare into his eyes said that she admired him so much and inside there was a yearning for far more.

But they had grown up together since grade school and in many ways had been more like brother and sister. Susan had often thought that she could make the transition, but sensed that Lenard probably could not do so.

Lillian's gown was a lovely light peach color and it blended so well with her hair and brown eyes. She wore a white band about her head that had just a touch of lace and held her hair back somewhat but otherwise allowed it flow down along the sides of her face. Her eyes were bright and she appeared as a living goddess.

David wore an open white shirt, dark blue sports coat and light tan slacks, and looked charming in his own right. He was adept at dancing and guided Lillian across the floor with considerable skill.

During the dance, Lenard did his best to pay attention to Susan, and most often did. But his eyes kept wondering toward Lillian more than once in a while. He noticed that Lillian would occasionally glance his way, in more of a curious manner rather than a giving him a suggestion or invitation. But to him, she was observing him and that was gratifying enough. His thoughts were racing ahead thinking of how great it will be when the time came for them to dance.

He took Susan with him as he approached Lillian and David knowing that protocol would require David to dance with Susan and that would separate him from Lillian. "May I have this dance Lillian," he asked. Lillian lit up with enthusiasm as she extended her hand and then withdrew somewhat as she glanced toward David. Lenard ignored the notion that David was not thrilled with this exchange.

But David's consolatory prize was not without beauty and grace, for Susan was an attractive girl, very pretty, had wide eyes and a love for life. She loved to tease and have fun.

As they glided across the floor, Lenard felt how well Lillian and he moved together. She seemed to anticipate his every move, and they flowed together as one. They chatted and laughed as the dance continued. He noticed that she was not taking glances at David but seemed to be perfectly comfortable in his arms.

Then gradually she grew somewhat distant, quieter, and nervous. Lenard was perplexed but continued with small talk so as to calm any uneasy thoughts that she may be having.

As the dance ended, Lenard offered "Lillian, I would like you to join me at my table. We can get to know each other." "Alright, but I don't want to upset Susan." "I don't think Susan will be upset," he replied. "She is a natural socialite. I'm sure she will be visiting several tables before the evening ends. She will be just fine."

Lenard held the chair for Lillian as she sat down. "Lenard you may call me Lilly if you'd like," With that, Lenard's smile broke into a wide grin. She could see that the informality was to Lenard's liking.

"I can see that Susan and you are very close," she suggested. "Yes, we are," replied Lenard, "We grew up together. She is like a kid sister to me." Lenard was pleased to clear the air about his relationship with Susan.

"And you are very close to David also?" Lenard inquired. "Yes," she said as she broke into a chuckle, "He is like a big brother to me." The conversation seemed to end there, and for next couple of minutes they sat there being a little awkward toward each other.

Lillian had noticed Ruby sitting to Lenard's back at a table some distance away. She kept looking his way far more often than Lillian liked. And her eyes seemed to shine green with envy. Lillian realized that Lenard was indeed a well sought after man and perhaps the most sought after man in the entire area. Not only that, but there was something about Lenard that Lillian could not quite place her finger on but had her finding a deep curiosity and interest in him.

It was settling for Lillian to see that David and Susan were enjoying each other's company. She could see that Susan was very outgoing, engaging and full of laughter. And they danced almost every dance. However, she did not like Ruby's continual interest in the man that was supposed to be giving her his attention for the remainder of the evening.

Finally, Lillian spoke of herself, "Well Lenard, I am just a plain small-town girl. I have brown eyes and light hair and some people think I am pretty." Lenard liked the idea that she was talking about herself. He also read this as making a case for herself. "Yes," he said, "Lilly, you are not only pretty but beautiful." He was also thinking that Lillian was genuine and wholesome and exactly what he wanted.

But then, the tables turned on him. Lillian offered, "I do not have red hair and I'm not overly flirtatious and fancy like some of your friends." Although she did not say it, Lenard knew to whom she was referring. There was no question as to the meaning of her remark.

After a moment, Lenard reached over and took her hand. Then he spoke softly as his blue eyes focused on hers. "Well Lilly, I guess you are right, I could be anywhere I wanted to be right now." At that moment, his eyes seemed to pierce hers and found a way into the outer edges of her soul. This never-before experience for her was unnerving and somewhat frightening.

She allowed his intrusion to continue for a few moments attempting to understand what was happening, and then broke it off by glancing away. But even through all that, she recognized the significance of what he had said to her - that he indeed chose to be there with her.

They continued to sit together and chat for the remainder of the evening as the towns folks took to the floor and danced. And they danced once in a while. Lenard enjoyed having her sole attention, almost to the extent of creating the impression that she was his and he was hers.

But Lillian still had lingering thoughts of Susan's and Ruby's interest in him, and how the eye contact with him had left her unbalanced and wondering about herself. She wasn't used to being anything but cool, calm, and collected. And she was no pushover when it came to men.

Although Lillian interacted with him pleasantly for the remainder of the evening, she spoke infrequently. She seemed to be somewhat distant and uncomfortable. Lenard was perplexed by this downturn when everything before that had gone so well. They walked to her car holding hands casually without saying anything. The evening ended with Lenard's unsolicited promise to call her the next day.

Chapter 4. The Interview

The next day I had an interview with Gerald Walker, the young upstart politician. He covered his life since childhood, starting with his mother and father being Margret and Carl Walker. His parents and grandparents had been residents of Maytown all their lives. He was a terrific athlete and scholar and had won the Governor's award for accomplishments at the age of thirteen. He had been selected as an academic, all-state running back and ended up playing football for an ivy-league school in the East. He was repeatedly voted in as President of his college class. He was personable and charming.

MISS DAISY

His current bid for U. S. Senator was thought to be far ahead of his closest competitor. The election was still months away in November but all indications were that he would win by a great margin.

Underneath it all, he appeared to be highly motivated and driven. I noted that he did not spend a term or two in the House of Representatives, but was campaigning directly for Senator.

I asked about an eventual bid for President of the United States. He grinned and indicated that time will tell. It was clear that this young man was very ambitious and could handle himself well with regard to being questioned and other affairs.

The interview left me with mixed thoughts about the people of this town. Perhaps they weren't as robotic as I had thought. But a lingering question remained. How could this young man evolve into such an outgoing, upstanding, polished young man so rapidly in just four years at an eastern college?

Perhaps there was more to the townspeople than meets the eye. But I was convinced that he was an exception, because as far as I was concerned these people definitely would have difficulty making it in the outside world.

Well, I had the main part of my story. I could now see what Watson was talking about and also that, not if but when, this young man ran for president I would have the inside track.

The bad news for me would be that I might have to come to Maytown often to cover his campaign activities. I thought that perhaps his advancements may mean that I would be able to do my job elsewhere - perhaps Washington DC as he moved up the political ladder.

I went back to the hotel and began to write the story. I noted that there were many gaps and that I would have to stay the weekend to fill in missing parts. Also I had not obtained a thorough enough background for the young man and a feel for the town of his upbringing. I would spend time here until Monday when I'd drive back to Bennington to get the train home.

Chapter 5. Pursuit of Each Other.

The next day Lenard called Lillian as promised. He was hoping to get a positive response from her, but she seemed not to be in an engaging mood, but not unwilling to talk either. There was something definitely interfering with Lenard's pursuit of Lillian. His thoughts about what it might be and why kept racing through his head as he tried to make sense of this dilemma.

Lenard imagined that Lillian having seen David's interest in Susan may have been upsetting when she had time to think about it. Probably she wasn't sure of her emotions about that, and was reluctant to let go of David.

Lenard also thought that she could not help noticing Susan's interest in him, although he believed that was squared away at the dance. She also could be

Fred Grace

upset about Ruby pretending that things were developing between her and him. He was having difficulty figuring out Lillian's reactions. Lenard was unaware that her deep attraction for him was causing her to be scared and unsure of herself.

Lillian was terrified of moving too fast toward Lenard, because she knew that she would fall deeply and hopelessly in love. And how would he react? Would she be just another passing fancy along the way like Ruby? Was he just biding his time before turning back to Susan? And, would she be able to recapture David's interest? At this point, Lillian was a woman in "no man's land."

As the phone conservation ended, Lenard persuaded Lillian to meet him at the park in Maytown. He arrived early and sat on a park bench near a fountain. As she came into view and continued toward him, his feelings for her intensified. His hopes were that she would feel as strongly about him.

As she approached, Lenard called out "Hello Lilly. I am so happy to see you." "Hi Lenard. Were you waiting long? I didn't mean to make you wait." "No dear," Lenard responded, "I got here a little early." "It's such a beautiful day, don't you think?" "Yes it is," was Lenard's reply. Lenard noticed that she seemed relaxed and in a talkative mood.

She sat down on the park bench beside him facing the fountain. As they sat there, waves of light mist would flow over them with alternating showers of sunlight to warm their faces. And too, it seemed as if the water was doing a dance just for them.

26

In the midst of all this, she exclaimed, "Lenard, You have chosen such a wonderful spot for us to meet!" "Well Lilly, I am not familiar with this park, but when I saw the fountain, I thought you might enjoy it." "Yes, it is lovely," she responded.

Lillian really liked Lenard and more than that, that unforgettable experience of his gazing into her eyes told her she was ready to become deeply involved. If she had to make a decision that very day she would without question say "Yes!" Sitting beside her, he seemed so warm and gentle. And his eyes were so blue, focused, and inviting. And she wondered how long it would be before she would fall hopelessly in love with him.

"What will you be doing now that the tennis season is over," Lenard asked. "Well, I'll be concentrating on my studies. Final exams are coming up," was Lillian's response. "And, we are getting ready for our spring presentation, so I'll be busy with choir rehearsals." "I guess I'll be doing the same," Lenard offered.

"So you like to sing?" he asked. "I do, and you?" "Yes, I do too. Do you know the song 'Play a Simple Melody'?" Lenard inquired. She nodded. Lenard started it off and she joined in. They took turns singing the rounds. The song ended in laughter as they both realized not only how much fun they were having, but also perhaps an inkling of how much fun they could have with each other in the days to come.

"Lenard," Lillian declared, "You have a great voice." "And so do you, my dear. We could become a famous duo!" And they laughed about that. He had a wry sense of humor that just struck the right note to create deep lingering chuckles within her.

Lenard related that his ambition was to become an architectural engineer. Lillian told him that she wanted to be a math teacher and tennis instructor. They sat there together exchanging dreams for quite some time.

As they sat together, Lenard engaged her with "Lilly, when I first saw you on the tennis court, I could not stop thinking about you and how beautiful you are." "Lenard," she admitted, "You caught my eye and I felt an attraction that I never experienced before. Perhaps you felt that I was being coy, but I was treading lightly since I was not sure if you felt the same way".

Lenard leaned toward her and said "Lilly you are the most beautiful woman I've ever met and I feel we can have a great life together." She responded with an instinctive unabridged motion toward him and exclaimed "Oh Lennard," as she threw her arms about him. In the midst of this gesture, she realized that this overt reaction toward him could not be reversed.

Lenard took advantage of her inadvertent move toward him and drew her even closer. He looked deeply into her eyes. He observed that as her eyes closed, she became nearly breathless, and then raised her face toward him. The two embraced as they held each other tightly in each other's arms. Then, Lenard whispered softly in her ear, "I Love You!"

Chapter 6. Hopelessly in Love

For the next week, Lillian would replay falling in love with Lenard without any thoughts of her once founded fears. She had thrown caution to the wind and now was fully engulfed. And she was constantly mesmerized by images of the fountain, the mist, splashes of sunlight, and water dancing in front of her very eyes.

She would replay being held in his arms, their first embrace and her feelings as he told her he loved her. And she seemed to light up at the very thought of him, glide across the floor on tiptoes as it seemed, and was filled with wonderment. These compelling signs could be recognized by anyone who even casually noticed. She was in love.

Fred Grace

Lillian would have to face up to telling David of her new found love, not wanting to hurt him but none-the-less wanting him to know. She knew that David seemed to have an interest in Susan, but wasn't sure if anything was to come of it. She called David by phone. "David, I have something I need to tell you. But before I do, I'd like to know what you are thinking about Susan."

David apologized saying "I should have told you sooner that Susan and I have become very serious about each other. I am very fond of her." "Do you feel that Susan will love you and want to be with you forever?" she asked. "Yes," David replied, "I do." "Well, I am glad you have found someone David. I think she is a great gal and I am happy for you."

Lillian was relieved that David's interests were focused on Susan and they would be together. This situation gave her the freedom to love Lenard completely without any estranged feelings toward her by David.

Lillian hesitated then went on "I want you to know that I have fallen in love with Lenard. I hope you can understand." "Yes, I suspected that that would happen. Lenard is a great guy and a fierce competitor," offered David. "And don't forget I'll always be your friend."

The following year while Lillian was still in school Lenard would come to Maytown each weekend to court Lillian. They were having the time of their lives. They would take short trips together, he accompanied her to school dances and affairs, and he would attend her tennis matches rooting of course for his favorite player.

On occasion, they would visit the park and gaze at the fountain, sometimes not saying much but letting the sounds of the water speak for them as they gazed into each other's eyes. And sometimes they would sing some old songs just for fun.

In late spring she graduated and took a job in the department store downtown. It was at that time they laid plans for a wedding.

Chapter 7. About Town

I accepted the idea that I would be stuck in Maytown for the weekend. I took note that the town fair was not to begin until next week so I resigned myself to writing, walking about town, and marking time. I went to the park during a break from writing and noticed that the townspeople had taken great care in creating and preserving the park.

I stood in front of a rather large stone that was covered with a bronze placard. I read a few names of those brave men who had given their lives during World War II. It struck me that there was at least one aspect of rural life that was in common with the big city. The heroes of the war were respected everywhere in the country.

Then going down the list of names, I found Carl Walker, Born Feb 21, 1918, and Died August 6, 1944. I recalled my interview with the young man who had scarcely made reference to his father, and then seemingly only when he was very young. During much of our conversations he talked mostly about his mother. This new finding would become an interesting aspect of my story.

As I turned to roam a bit more in the park, I heard music coming from a couple hundred yards away. It was a band composed of adults playing "Yankee Doddle Dandy." A small group of townspeople were attending what appeared to me to be an almost unremarkable event. But they seemed to be enjoying themselves.

I thought that the song was further evidence of the folks being behind in time. It had been around since the revolutionary war and by now was sung mostly by children. A couple of other songs were also terribly dated. I resigned myself to the idea that this is the way life is in these parts.

I left the park and roamed about town. I was surprised that the downtown buildings seemed relatively new, and that business apparently was doing well. I could see that some buildings of three and four stories loomed large in this town and stood tall above others that were either one or two stories.

The downtown consisted of about four square blocks and there was a rather large fountain in the center of the main intersection. The few cars that passed by would make a circle about the intersection's center and then proceed on their way.

Apparently, the town had one taxi and it stood idle at one corner of the intersection. A patrol car was parked across the street on another corner. I saw the local policeman walking leisurely in the direction of the hotel, then he disappeared into a coffee shop.

I stood next to one of the tallest buildings that was a department store of more modern style. I noticed a dry cleaning store across the street. On down the street at some distance was a one-story building that housed the local newspaper office. I crossed the street and walked on down to get a first-hand look.

The large plate glass window contained the paper's name in gold letters with thin black trim. The large letters were displayed in an arc and identified the newspaper as "The Maytown Sentinel." As I peered through the window, I saw the press sitting toward the back of the main room. It appeared quite old, and I thought it to be the type that Ben Franklin might have used for printing "Poor Richard's Almanac."

There was a diner on one corner and a two-story bank on the opposite corner. A jewelry store sat next to the bank. Beyond that, a woman's clothing store stood sandwiched between a hardware store and another small restaurant. There was a movie theater in the middle of the second block. The marquee read "Hello Dolly."

A few stores beyond that was a storefront that was being used as a temporary political office. I chose to walk toward it since it caught my curiosity. Apparently, an opponent for the U. S. Senate was a man named Allen

Green. I made a mental note to visit this office later to inquire about my young politician's competitor.

As I walked along back to the hotel, I noticed the wildly contrasting differences between this backward town and the big city. I was beginning to sense that the town did have a certain amount of charm in ways and appeared to be self-sustaining.

While life was quite simple here, there was some evidence of people having a fulfilled life and purpose. I began to wonder if there was another existence not without merit that I had completely missed and had not been exposed to during my short life thus far on this planet.

Chapter 8. Unfulfilled Promise.

After graduation, Lillian took a job downtown in the local department store where she worked for Mr. Cline, the store's owner. Her job was sales lady in the women's clothing department. She had a good eye for fashion and was very helpful to the ladies who frequented the store.

But she was good at math and fast with numbers so she soon found herself working directly for Mr. Cline in the accounting office. Cline and his wife had no children and she soon found herself becoming his adopted daughter, so to speak. Cline would give visiting salesmen the wary eye when he noticed their unusual interest in Lillian. He would give the more aggressive ones a stern warning that she was his daughter and they had better not be bothering her, or else. This was an ideal situation for Lillian because she wanted no parts of the men who came traipsing through the office.

Letters from Lenard kept her going. She would read and reread them for comfort during his absence. Otherwise she would go to work, walk about town, enjoy what she could of town activities, the yearly fair, and occasional concerts held at the park.

She attended David and Susan's wedding and although she was happy for them, there was an emptiness within her while Lenard was away. But she kept going day to day by Lenard's letters, his love for her, and knowing that they were to get married as soon as he returned.

As time wore on she found herself reading romance novels and dreaming of her day when her prince would come. She became less involved in the community but continued to be diligent in her work. The news that Susan gave birth to a son was met with mixed emotions. Although she was to be his godmother, she felt like life was passing her by.

She felt even more distraught when Susan related that David had taken a position in the east and they would be leaving town soon. She became lonely and more withdrawn, but knew her time would come when Lenard came home.

Every time the telephone rang she would jump to answer it hoping it would be good news from Lenard. After many, many calls, she began to wonder if his call would ever come. His letters were not so frequent now since he was in the war zone. Sometimes a month would go by and although she wrote letters to him every week she could not be sure he actually had received them.

She awoke early that morning to the ring of the telephone. The sun was just coming up and in her drowsiness she wondered who in the world could be calling at this time. It was Lenard! She was so overwhelmed that she could hardly speak.

"Lilly my love, I have great news. I am being discharged and will be home soon. I'll be taking the train form the west coast to Chicago and then driving to Maytown. I'll call you from the hotel the moment I get there." "Oh Lenard, I've been waiting for you for so long. Do you still love me?" she asked. "Of course I do, my love. I'll always love you."

"How have you been my dear?" She related how lonely she has been being there without him and that only his letters kept her going over the past three years. Lenard stated "Your waiting is over sweetheart. I will be home in a few days."

Lenard had been called up in the draft by the Army. He left his older foster parents in Springdale and took the train from Bennington to Ft. Oak in the eastern part of the country. There he went through basic training and was sent to the war front.

Each week he would receive letters from Lillian and she would receive letters from him. He would relay that he was often put in danger, but would comfort her by saying that he will come home soon and be with her for the rest of their lives.

In his last letter, he related that his tour of duty was over and he soon would be discharged from the service. As he had said on the phone later, he would call her and let her know exactly when he would begin his journey home. Later he would call her from the Maytown Hotel and have her meet him there. She would not wait for his call from the Hotel. From the dates he had given, Lillian figured that she would be waiting at the Hotel to be there when he arrived on Saturday a week later.

Lillian came to the hotel wearing an off-white dress. She had dreamed of this day for years and she looked as lovely as a spring bride. She entered the hotel and took a seat in the lobby so as to keep the entrance in view. She was thrilled beyond comparison that her prince would soon be coming through the large front door of the hotel lobby. She waited and waited but Lenard did not come. She returned the next day but also no Lenard. She spent the week going to the hotel each day but each time she was sorely disappointed. Lenard did not come.

Lillian wrote letters to his parents in Springdale but those were returned marked with "addressee unknown." In her search for him she learned that Lenard's foster parents had passed and no one lived there anymore. Her pursuit of him came to a dreadful end.

Chapter 9. Our Encounter.

It was Saturday morning. The sidewalk in Maytown was quite busy as I walked along. I was headed for the same coffee shop that the policeman had visited up the block. In the distance, among others approaching, my eyes were drawn to a particular woman whose off-white dress was lit by the morning sun.

She kept going in and out of view as others walked between us but glimpses told me that she was an elegant woman of perhaps thirty-five or so. She was indeed a Lady with every stitch in place, her hair was back and partially covered with a modest laced net, and she walked erect and with a certain unsettling confidence.

I became curious about this woman so I picked a path that would keep us in view of each other. It seemed that she too had picked me out and was looking my way. As we got closer her brown eyes seemed to widen and there was little doubt in my mind that she indeed was focused on me.

As we became still closer her eyes fell to the side then raised again but were gazing beyond me. As we passed, I turned my head to get a close look. Her face had a certain perplexing shine that seemed to linger from her youth. I thought to myself, what a beautiful Lady this woman has been.

After entering the coffee shop, I engaged a middle aged man with the idea that he may know who she is. "I really don't know but some say she was a resident in this town before the fire." "What fire?" I asked. "The one in 1956 that wiped out most of the town's buildings," he replied. "They say she left Maytown after the fire. In fact nearly all the people who worked downtown left afterwards to find work elsewhere."

"What is her name," I inquired. "They call her Miss Daisy but nobody knows why." "Miss Daisy," I muttered to myself. He repeated, "Miss Daisy, that's right. She comes here for about a week each year, stares into the jewelry store window for a while each day, and then goes to the park. After that she leaves town."

As I took sips of coffee, I found myself becoming even more curious about this lady. I reflected on our encounter. Why was she looking at me so intently? Maybe I reminded her of someone. Yes, someone she expected to see. Could she have thought that I was her chosen one? Was he killed in the fire? Perhaps not for if so she would not be searching. My mind was exploding with notions, none of which made total sense. I decided to go to the park and attempt to find out.

I found her sitting quietly on a park bench facing a mid-sized fountain. The silence in the air was broken only by the water falling over the edges of the fountain. Her loneliness was more than apparent. I sat beside her without saying anything for some time. Then, I spoke softly to her. "I am curious about you Miss Daisy. Do you mind?" She nodded without looking my way.

After a few minutes, she raised her hand and offered an old faded book. Although its cover was worn, its title seemed to be reminiscent of a romance novel. It fell open at the page containing the marker and my eyes moved quickly to a dried flower. It was a daisy with all but one petal having been plucked. Beneath the flower was a hand written note that said "He loves me not."

I sat there pondering the daisy that meant so much to her. It was clear that she knew the meaning of plucking that last petal and had not removed it. After some time, she turned her head slightly toward me and ask "Who are you?" and then went back to staring at the fountain. "My name is Johnathan," I replied. As she lipped my name, her face seemed to warm as if something about me had inspired a warm feeling inside.

We sat together for long time without saying anything else. As I left, I wanted to say "Goodbye for now, Miss Daisy," but not wanting to lead her into thinking that I might return, I just said "Goodbye, Miss Daisy."

After leaving her, I thought of how sad it was for her to be caught up in such a situation. A situation that seemed to me that had nothing to do with being from a small town or large city. A situation that I could not completely comprehend. Perhaps it was only when she came to Maytown that she became withdrawn, but I really couldn't be sure. Perhaps she was fully functional and relatively happy otherwise.

I was torn with conflicting possibilities – her beauty, her sadness, her loneliness, and what appeared to be a never ending fruitless quest. And I was surprised by my own reaction to her. I was demanding that someone do something. I wrestled during the night with a dilemma. Why me? Why not brush Miss Daisy aside without thought as I had probably done a hundred times before? But I could not do so.

I awoke the next day and decided to get my news story finished and leave pursuit of Miss Daisy until Monday when the Library was open. Yes, I wanted to follow up on Miss Daisy, not as a reporter seeking a story, but because this newly found strange curiosity in me was compelling me to do so.

I felt an unusual sense of compassion that was foreign to the hardened reporter that I had become. I immediately canceled my train reservation for Monday that would have taken me home.

Monday morning came and again I headed for the coffee shop. A woman of about thirty-some years sat beside me at the counter. After some small talk, I asked if she knew Miss Daisy. "Yes," she replied and then went on, "I knew her when we were in grade school. Then we moved away. I came back to live here only a few years ago. I tried to befriend her but got no response. As I recall, her real name is Lillian. I've been told that she was jilted by some guy who left and never returned."

I put down my coffee cup, immediately bolted out the door, and headed for the Library. As I walked along, I thought about how rude I had been to the woman without a thank you or goodbye. It surprised me that I even gave that a thought, because I had never been so considerate in the past.

At the Library I dug into the school year books and found her. Lillian Marsh, graduating class of 1952, academic, choir, tennis 4 years, and prom queen in her senior year. Her picture revealed her captivating beauty in her youth. I paused looking at her picture and thought of how age did not steal away her beauty. She was still a beautiful woman.

From there, I rushed to the old newspaper section and began scouring the news of the day. There it was. Saturday, April 11th, 1953, "Lillian Marsh engaged to Lenard Trussel." I frantically searched the pages for Lenard but found nothing.

Chapter 10. Trip to Harpersville

I would not let the unknown whereabouts of Lenard cause my pursuit to become a dead end. I headed straight for the courthouse. As I searched birth records of the state, I came across Lenard Trussel, born August 1931 in Springdale, which was about an hour's drive from here.

My heart was pounding as I drove along the old road from Maytown to Springdale. My mind was working overtime, and I just could not stop thinking about getting to the bottom of what now was becoming an obsession.

Lenard was listed in the yearbook of 1951, academic, choir, and tennis 4 years. The tennis part was a significant coincidence. From his picture I could see that he was a handsome sort and noticed a strong resemblance to me, although I never thought of myself as being handsome. I had other attributes like the gift of gab and writing.

But where was Lenard now? I searched the old newspapers for many hours. The papers were plastered with stories related to the fire in the neighboring town. Then finally on the back page of one edition I found a chilling article. Lenard Trussel, age 23, was in an accident on his way home after discharge from the service. It went on to say that he lost almost all memory of things in his life before that time.

At a coffee shop, I talked to a man who was about the age of Lenard. "Yes, I knew him briefly. They say he lives in Harpersville at the other end of the state."

I left Springdale and headed to Harpersville. As I drove along, it began to rain like crazy. The trip seemed to be endless. I could not listen to the radio because there was so much static in the air. So I was left with the slapping of the wipers and my own thoughts to keep my mind busy. There were no other cars on the road and the road grew more desolate with each mile.

I noticed that the fuel gauge was low so I began to look for a gas station. I had forgotten to tank up. Such situation wasn't a problem in the big city since I usually took the subway or taxi to get about town. Finally, I could see a faint light in the distance. Yes, it was a small country station with two pumps out in front of a small shack.

Nobody seemed to be attending the pumps so I got out to do the job myself. Rain poured down over my broad-rimed hat and trench coat as I filled the tank. Finally, an old man appeared out of nowhere. I took it that he was the owner or attendant.

"What are you doing out on a night like this?" He asked. "Heading for Harpersville," I replied. "Need to be careful. They say the storm is a bad one," he offered. "Do you need any oil," he asked. "No, I don't," was my answer. "How about your tires?" He inquired. "They should be alright - it's a rental." "All right, that will be four dollars and fifty cents." "How far is it to Springdale," I asked. "About a hundred miles," was his reply.

As I got back into the car, I thought about Watson sending me on a wild goose chase was not good enough for me. Oh no, I had to create my own goose chase that was far worse. The storm had brought leaves and small branches down from the trees along the road and these were strewn everywhere. It was so dark and with the rain pouring down I could hardly see the road.

Somehow, my mind was conjuring up a vision of a tree that had fallen across the road. I was harkening back to the old horse operas that I had seen as a kid where a tree had fallen across the trail and the wagon men had to dislodge it before continuing. Yes, for some of them, their search for a better life in the west might have been a pursuit of folly to some extent but my pursuit of Lenard seemed to be total folly. But there was no tree and no excuse for me to abandon my journey.

I thought that if Watson knew about this crazy adventure, he would be having the laugh of his life. He wouldn't fault me for pursuing Miss Daisy, but would be howling about the predicament I had gotten myself into and the wiggling and squirming I was doing.

But this was not Watson's doing. It was mine. I knew that this outing was nothing but crazy and questioned my sanity. I needed to see a shrink. Why in the world did I allow myself to be dragged into such quagmire? Why was I being so stupid? I concluded that this pursuit was one that I would have to give up on. Miss Daisy would be left for someone else to pursue, not me. I turned around and headed back to Springdale.

As I approached the station again, I pulled over and parked in front of the pumps, wipers going, engine running, and headlights on. After a few minutes, the old man came out and knocked on the window. "Is anything wrong?" he asked. "No, I just decided to go back to Springdale," I replied. He responded with "That's probably a good idea."

"Would you like a coffee?" "Yes, I would. Black if you don't mind." In a few moments he returned with the coffee. "If you'd like you can park over there for the night," he suggested. "What do I owe you?" "Nothing," he replied, "I should have offered you one before." "Well thanks, but I need to be moving along."

Chapter 11. Pursuit of Lenard

As I began to pull out onto the road, I found myself hesitating with my foot on the brake. I sat there for several minutes in a quandary. Then, my arrogance and pride began to take over. Pride, that's what it is. Pride was the quality that had made me a successful reporter but now had turned on me and became a scourge. I realized that perhaps my pride is why Watson sent me here in the first place. He knew me well. He knew that I would not stop digging until I got to the very bottom of things.

Fred Grace

By then, the rain let up somewhat and I took that as an omen. I decided to make a U-turn and go to Harpersville after all. As I went along, I felt like a feeble earthling attempting to do the job of angels seriously working to obtain wings.

I awoke to the sun shining into my eyes through the windshield. At first, I wondered where I was and why. I often did that when traveling, especially when tired and the pace was hectic. I noticed that the rain had ceased but the sidewalk and street were still wet. And I was in good luck. Inadvertently, I had parked in front of a small restaurant. Then, it came to me. Harpersville - I am here to find Lenard.

I felt beat and ragged as I got out of the car. I entered the restaurant and went directly to the restroom where I splashed my face with water and combed my hair. I returned and after having glanced about, I decided to sit at the counter.

The waitress dressed in a plain light yellow dress with a white apron approached and asked, "Black or white," referring to whether I wanted cream in my coffee or not. "Black," I replied. She handed me a menu and suggested some breakfast specials. I said "No, thanks. I'll just have coffee and a breakfast roll."

An older man sat at the other end of the counter. Two women were sitting in one of the booths and three guys were in the next booth. I overheard them talking about local, state, and national politics. I noticed that they had quite a different take, and didn't appear to be that well informed. I chalked it up to the small town and that that's the way it must be out here in the boondocks.

As I sat there attempting to get awake, my mind was slowly returning to my purpose. I turned about and asked "Does anyone know the whereabouts of Lenard Trussel?" After comparing notes, one of the men offered that he lives in a small white house at the end of Maple Street. I thanked him, chugged the coffee, and hurried down the street as fast as I could as if he might not live there anymore.

A man came to the door. His stature was nearly six feet, he had an athletic build and could have passed easily for my father or older brother. I noticed a faint scar on his forehead extending down slightly below the hairline. "Mr. Trussel?" I inquired. "Yes, I am Lenard Trussel," he replied. "What do you want?"

I explained that I was interested in his accident and that I wanted to talk to him about it. He indicated that others had talked to him but he could tell them very little. I informed him that I might have some information about his life before the accident. He invited me in, sat me in a chair directly across from him, and we talked.

I asked if he had friends and who they might be. He informed me that he often goes fishing with several married guys, and kind of joked that he was their excuse for getting out of the house. He mentioned that all the town folks get together on Thursday nights to dance.

I asked if he had a girlfriend or a wife. He shared with me that he dances with some fine ladies but somehow something seemed to be missing. Then added that he doesn't know why but just never had any deep interest in them beyond having some fun and friendship. No, he had never been married.

51

"Do you remember Springdale?" I asked. "Yes, faintly," he replied. "I remember being there and living with an old man and woman. They are gone now, but I go back to Springdale a couple of times a year and walk about town."

"Some people seem to know me and greet me as we pass on the street, but I don't really know who they are. I keep going back thinking there is something lost or that something might trigger my mind to things that happened in those days."

I followed up with "And how about High School, do you remember anything?" "No, not a lot, except I do have lingering images of playing tennis," was his answer. I told him that I had some pictures of him playing tennis and asked if he would like to see them. He nodded affirmatively.

I showed him the one of mixed doubles. "That's me alright and there's that other guy – the kid had a great serve." I wanted to point out Lillian in the back of the opposite court but decided to use a different approach.

"Do you remember Maytown," I asked. "Seems to me we had tennis matches with them," he responded. "Does a girl named Lillian mean anything to you?" I asked. "Lilly," he declared as his face took on a somewhat puzzled look. I knew from the contraction that her name had struck a nerve.

Then just as quickly, his face became sullen and distant. He wanted to know what happened. But before giving an answer, I wanted to know how much was coming back to him so I carefully asked a few more questions.

"Did you know Lilly?" I asked. "Why yes," he answered after some hesitation. "Seems she was a beautiful girl with light brown hair, brown eyes, and was the fairest of them all." Then he offered, "That's strange." He paused for a few moments and then continued. "To this day I have a reoccurring dream of a girl floating and dancing about me – and I have wondered who she is. Could it be that she is Lilly?"

Then he went on to say with more certainty "Yes, that's it, she is Lilly." His face grew sullen again and he struggled to hold back tears. Eventually, he related that after his discharge he was to meet her at the Hotel in Maytown. He added that she didn't know exactly when he was coming home. That part was to be a surprise.

After a long pause he asked with a shaky voice "You are here to tell me about Lilly, aren't you?" I replied, "Only if you want to know." He began to sob and nodded.

I knew that my words would have to be chosen carefully at this delicate moment. I waited and finally said "Lilly is waiting for you Lenard. She doesn't know about the accident – thinks you didn't love her, yet she goes to Maytown each year hoping you would come back to her."

As he began to remember more of her, his eyes became laden with moisture, his heart was heavy, and pain was etched into his face. After some time, he regained his composure, wiped his eyes, and added that he wanted to see her.

Fred Grace

As we drove to Maytown, I filled him in on Lilly being referred to by the townspeople as Miss Daisy and all of that. He didn't say much but once in a while he would sob for a few moments. I was acutely aware that my actions were causing brutal pain within Lenard even though they were of the best intentions.

Chapter 12. Consummation

We arrived in Maytown late Thursday morning. The wet sidewalks and streets were nearly dry now from the sun shining brightly in the clear blue sky. I left Lenard off at the Hotel and parked across the street to be out of the way and to watch.

As he left the hotel, I saw Lillian coming up the street in her off-white dress as before. As they approached each other, her chin lifted and I knew she was thinking that she had seen him. But suddenly she stopped. I thought "Oh no, this may not turn out well." I was used to reporting stories but not creating them.

But Lenard had seen her also and kept moving toward her. He reached out with his sturdy arms and she responded by lifting her arms feebly toward him. I was relieved realizing that her sudden stop came from being overwhelmed. They met with an embrace as he lifted her off her feet. I closed my eyes for a moment to capture what I had just seen. Then, I watched as they headed slowly to the park.

I found a spot away from the fountain so as not to be noticed but wanted them in view. Through the mist and falling water, I could see their colored figures sitting close and holding hands. I could hear mixtures of voices, sobs, and tearful laughter. And amidst interruptions of laughter, I heard them singing some sort of old song that had something to do with "a simple melody."

I waited for quite a while to give them time together before approaching. With wet eyes, Lenard stood, shook my hand, and gave me a long solid hug. Then Lilly extended her hand and I took her hand in mine. My eyes grew moist as I addressed her for the first time as "Lilly." "Jonathan," she said as she smiled at me through her tear-stained face, "From first you spoke to me, I wondered if you were to be my Angel."

As I left them, I wasn't sure about this Angel thing but had to admit that my interest in Miss Daisy had led me to a fuller understanding of compassion. I had to acknowledge that Miss Daisy, perhaps unknowingly, had changed me significantly. Then a sobering thought struck me that Miss Daisy had been my Angel.

MISS DAISY

On occasion as years passed and when traveling through the countryside, I would stop and count petals of daisies, wondering what the answer would be and if anything could be done to change the outcome. And each time, I would smile deeply within myself about that question. And I often thought, thank you Miss Daisy, for because of you, I have found the story of a lifetime. There is no story greater than that of Love.

Fred Grace

Additional Books by the Author:

Understanding Music Chord Structures and Progressions, Fred I. Grace, July 2016.

The Christmas Jack, Fred I. Grace, November 1986.

Visit: www.musicexplorers.com

www.ingramcontent.com/pod-product-compliance
Lightning Source LLC
Chambersburg PA
CBHW071213130626
46555CB00004B/1688